Dilly

SAVES THE DAY

D0993516

SAVES THE DAY

(PREVIOUSLY PUBLISHED AS
DILLY AND THE VAMPIRE)

TONY BRADMAN

ILLUSTRATED BY SUSAN HELLARD

For Gill, Greg, Dan and Isobel
from their favourite dinosaur

First published in Great Britain 1995
by Heinemann Young Books
under the title Dilly and the Vampire
Published 1996 by Mammoth
Reissued 1999 by Mammoth
an imprint of Egmont Children's Books Limited
239 Kensington High Street, London W8 6SA

Text copyright © 1995 Tony Bradman
Illustrations copyright © 1995 Susan Hellard
Cover illustration copyright © 1999 Susan Hellard

The moral rights of the author and illustrator have been asserted.

ISBN 0 7497 3796 4

10 9 8 7 6 5 4 3 2 1

A CIP catalogue record for this title
is available from the British Library

Printed in Great Britain
by Cox & Wyman Ltd, Reading, Berkshire

CONTENTS

DILLY AND THE VAMPIRE

'It's time to make your mind up, Dilly, once and for all,' said Mother the other week. 'Just who *is* coming with us on your birthday outing? I want four names and I want them . . . *now*.'

Mother and Father had told Dilly months ago they would take him somewhere special for a birthday treat, and that he could bring some friends along. Dilly simply had to decide who to invite.

Seems easy-peasy, doesn't it? Well, it wasn't. He'd changed his mind so much he'd nearly driven Mother and Father mad.

'But . . .' Dilly started to say. Mother

narrowed her eyes a fraction and Dilly got the message. 'OK,' he said quickly. 'Darryl, and Dudley and . . . no, not Dudley, I'll have Daniel and Dicky – but he doesn't like Darryl, so *he* can't come, and then there's . . .'

'STOP!' shouted Mother. She held a paw to her forehead. 'That's it, I've had enough. We'll take Darryl, Dudley and Daniel,' she declared. 'And we mustn't forget . . . Denzil.'

'*Denzil*?' said Dilly. 'But why does it have to be him?'

'Because he invited you on *his* birthday outing, dozy,' I said from behind Mother. 'So you have to invite him back.'

'Who asked you to butt in, smelly boots?' hissed Dilly.

'Actually, Dilly,' said Mother firmly, 'Dorla took the words out of my mouth. Besides, Denzil is a nice little dinosaur and he likes you a lot.'

'But I don't like *him*,' said Dilly. 'Everybody at school says he's a wimp.'

'Oh, do they?' said Mother. 'I suppose that's because he wears glasses and he's small for his age. You ought to be ashamed of yourself, Dilly. How often have I told you it's wrong to judge others by the way they look? I'll bet Denzil's got hidden depths.'

'Hidden *what*, Mother?' asked Dilly, sounding puzzled.

'Depths,' replied Mother. 'It means there might be more to Denzil than meets the eye.' Now Dilly was utterly baffled. 'Never mind,' sighed Mother. 'You mark my words, though. Denzil will surprise you and your friends one day . . . And he's coming on your outing. That's *final*.'

'But . . . but . . . it's not fair!' said Dilly scowling.

'Well, I'm afraid *I* think it is,' said Mother. 'So that's something we'll just have to disagree on, won't we?'

'Yes, Mother,' snapped Dilly. 'Can I go now?'

'You *may*,' said Mother.

Dilly stamped upstairs, STAMP, STAMP, STAMP. He went into his bedroom, paused, then slammed the door shut with a . . . BANG!

'I think that went quite well,' said Mother brightly, smiling through gritted teeth. 'Don't you agree, Dorla?'

I didn't, mostly because I thought it meant we were in for a Mammoth Dilly Sulking Session. But luckily, he soon cheered up.

At least he hadn't Dilly-dallied over where his outing should be. He had asked Mother and Father to take him to *The Count Dinula*

Experience. It's a special place for young dinosaurs based on the vampire film that was so popular last year, *Count Dinula, Prince of Bloodsuckers*.

I was looking forward to visiting it myself. Mother and Father had asked if I'd go along to help them and I'd said I would.

The big day came at last and we set off in the dino-car. Half an hour later, we parked near a spooky-looking black building. A huge neon sign on the front said: *The Experience*. Dilly couldn't wait and ran on ahead.

'Hi, guys!' we heard him yell.

Mother had arranged for Dilly's friends to meet us at the entrance, and they had already arrived. The parents asked what time they should collect their little dinosaurs and left.

I noticed that Darryl, Dudley and Daniel were almost as excited as Dilly. The four of them made an amazing amount of noise together.

Then I saw Denzil.

He didn't join in when the others gave Dilly the presents and cards they'd brought.

He stood slightly apart, trying to attract Dilly's attention. Father had to tap Dilly quite hard on the shoulder to make him turn round.

'Happy birthday, Dilly!' said Denzil, smiling nervously. He gave Dilly a neatly wrapped present and a large envelope. 'I hope you like the card. I spent the whole of yesterday making it.'

'Oh, thanks,' said Dilly, without much enthusiasm.

'It's probably a load of rubbish,' Darryl said. Dudley, Daniel and Dilly giggled. Denzil blushed bright green.

'I don't think we want any more comments like *that* this afternoon, Darryl,' said Mother. 'It's a *lovely* card, Denzil.'

Father put Dilly's presents and cards in the dino-car while Mother bought the tickets. Then we followed a crowd of chattering dinosaurs through the entrance and into a dark, dark chamber . . .

'Welcome to *The Count Dinula Experience*,' rumbled a deep voice. 'Step this way and prepare to be . . . TERRIFIED!'

A line of four-seater carriages came rattling in. Dilly leapt into the leading one with Darryl, Dudley and Daniel, leaving Denzil standing alone and uncertain. Mother took him by the paw.

'You can sit with us, Denzil,' she said, shooting Dilly a Wait-Till-I-Get-You-Home look. She climbed into the carriage behind with Denzil, and so did Father and I. The other carriages filled up . . . and off we went.

I've been on plenty of rides, but none as good as *The Count Dinula Experience*. The carriages slid slowly past scenes re-created from the film. I knew the whole thing was only dummies and sets and models and tape recordings and lights. Just the same, it was still pretty scary.

Thunder crashed and lightning flashed, doors creaked and bats squeaked, candles sputtered and voices muttered. There were ghastly goings-on in graveyards, and Count Dinula did lots of biting and sucking.

But of course, the biggest pain in the neck was . . . Dilly.

'I'm not frightened of you, stupid old Count Dinula!' he kept shouting. Darryl, Dudley and Daniel copied him, and soon all four were boasting loudly about how brave they were. Every so often they turned to snigger at Denzil. They were obviously convinced he was scared silly.

He wasn't though. And if you ask me, Dilly, Darryl, Dudley and Daniel *were* frightened. They were covering it up by showing off.

At the end of the ride, we found ourselves back in the dark, dark, chamber. Everybody headed for the exit, then stood outside in the street talking about how great it had been . . . and feeling relieved it was over.

Or was it? Suddenly, a shadow fell across the pavement. We looked round . . . and there was Count Dinula himself – *in the flesh*!' He had his cape raised like a pair of wings and his sharp fangs shone in the neon light.

'As you can see, there is no escape,' he said in his silky, evil, vampire voice. 'I will suck the blood of everybody here. And I shall begin with the littlest, juiciest ones first . . .'

I think most of us realised pretty quickly this wasn't a *real* vampire, only somebody made up to look like Count Dinula. The idea was to give everyone a last fright, just when we thought it was safe to relax.

I said *most* of us. Perhaps you can guess which small dinosaur and his chums stood rooted to the spot with horrified expressions on their faces.

Several things happened next, in quick succession.

Count Dinula advanced, and Darryl, Dudley and Daniel fled howling for their lives. Dilly opened his mouth instead and let rip with an ultra-special, 150-mile-per-hour super-scream, the kind that deafens a crowd of dinosaurs and stops pretend vampires dead in their tracks.

And Denzil surprised everybody.

'Don't worry, Dilly,' he yelled. 'I'll save you!'

Denzil dashed at the pretend Count Dinula, dived . . . and bit *him* on the ankle! The pretend Count Dinula yelped with pain and started hopping around. But whatever he did, he couldn't shake Denzil off . . .

It took ages for Father to prise open Denzil's jaws. Mother explained that Dilly wasn't in danger, and Denzil calmed down. He apologised and the pretend Count Dinula was nice enough to say he saw the funny side of it. I noticed he was limping quite badly as he walked away, though.

I also noticed Dilly was behaving rather

oddly. He was staring at Denzil as if he'd never really looked at him before, and he barely said goodbye to Darryl, Dudley and Daniel when their parents came to collect them.

And when it was Denzil's turn to leave, Dilly sidled up to him.

'Er . . . would you like to come round to my house some time, Denzil?' he said rather shyly, his tail tucked up under his bottom. 'I could show you my collection of squashed swamp slugs.'

Denzil seemed too happy to speak. He just grinned and nodded.

As we drove home afterwards, Mother, Father, Dilly and I kept going over what Denzil had done, and bursting into fits of laughter.

'I told you Denzil had hidden depths, Dilly,' said Mother, trying to be serious. 'Do you understand now what I meant?'

'Oh yes, Mother,' said Dilly eagerly. 'Do you think *I've* got any?'

'I sincerely hope not,' said Mother, a look of panic crossing her face.

And then we all burst into laughter again!

DILLY AND THE MISSING SWAMP-CHOCS

'How strange,' said Father. 'I can't seem to find the swamp-chocs we bought. Are they in any of those bags, dear?'

It was Saturday and we had just returned from the Dino-Market. I was helping Mother and Father unpack the shopping. Dilly wasn't. When we'd got home, he had trailed in last and gone straight up to his room.

'No, they're not,' said Mother. 'But I'm certain I put them in the top of a bag at the check-out. I hope we haven't dropped them somewhere . . .'

I felt the same. The swamp-chocs were

meant to be a treat for later. On Saturdays, Mother and Father usually buy something sweet for us all to share while we watch TV in the evening. And I adore swamp-chocs.

In fact, there's only one young dinosaur in the world who likes them more than me, and that's Dilly. Which is why I began to feel rather suspicious as Mother and Father searched and searched . . .

'Well, they're definitely not here,' said Father finally.

'I'll bet Dilly took them,' I said, unable to hold it in any longer.

Just at that moment, Dilly himself appeared in the kitchen doorway. I don't know whether he'd heard what I'd said. But suddenly he seemed to think of somewhere else he would rather be.

'That's not very fair, Dorla,' said Mother. 'I don't see how he could have. Dilly, you haven't been near the shopping, have you?'

Dilly froze. 'Who, me?' he replied. 'Er . . . no, Mother.'

I noticed he had blushed ever so slightly green. He had the oddest expression on his face, too . . . but then it vanished.

'You're lying,' I said. 'I can tell.'

'You shut up, stinky fat Dorla,' said Dilly crossly. 'You're only trying to get me into trouble with Mother and Father, just like you always do.'

'I do *not*,' I said. What a cheek!

'You do, you do!' yelled Dilly and began hopping up and down.

I yelled at him and we started a loud argument. Mother and Father told us to stop it, but we ignored them. Then the dino-phone rang.

'Right, that's enough!' bellowed Father, 'I'll count to five, and whoever's still shouting when I've finished won't get any pocket money. One . . .'

Dilly and I instantly went quiet. '*Thank you*,' said Father.

The call was from Donald, an old friend of Father's. It seemed Donald had moved back to Dino-Town, and would be visiting us later. Mother and Father were pleased . . . but Dilly and I weren't off the hook.

'You'd better both go to your rooms to cool off,' said Father. 'We don't want you behaving like a pair of hooligans when Donald's here.'

'But what about the swamp-chocs, Father?' I said.

'You'll just have to forget them, Dorla,' said Father.

'But . . .' I started to say.

'The subject is closed, Dorla,' said Mother firmly. 'Now up to your room and make sure you leave your little brother *alone*, OK?'

I pushed past Dilly who was giving me one of his Beat-You-This-Time smirks, stuck my snout in the air and went to my room.

I sat on my bed, brooding. I was absolutely convinced Dilly had taken the swamp-chocs, but I knew Mother and Father wouldn't believe me unless I could prove it. The question was . . . how?

I'd heard Dilly follow me upstairs and go into his room. But he didn't stay in it long. After ten minutes, I heard him heading downstairs again, probably to say he was sorry and generally be a creep.

'Now's my chance,' I thought. I could sneak into his room while he wasn't there and have a look in the usual hiding places. I eased my door open, checked no one was on the landing . . . and tippy-toed across.

'What *are* you doing, Dorla?' said a voice behind me.

I took a deep breath and turned round. Mother was coming out of the bathroom. She was holding some towels and giving me one of those stern parental stares, the kind that soon has you feeling incredibly guilty, even if you haven't done anything.

'Oh, I er . . . just wanted to make it up

with Dilly,' I said, flashing my biggest
I-Really-Am-*Such*-A-Sweet Dinosaur smile
at her. 'And after that I was, er . . . going to
come and say sorry to you and Father, of
course.'

'That's OK, then,' said Mother. 'But I
don't think you'll find Dilly in his room.

He's gone downstairs. I'm surprised you didn't hear him . . .'

'Drat,' I thought. It didn't look like I'd be able to slip into Dilly's room easily, so I would have to devise another plan. And I'd have to apologise to him, too, worse luck. There was no getting out of it now.

Dilly was in the sitting room with Father.

'Sorry, Dilly,' I said. 'Can we be friends?'

'Sure,' said Dilly. 'No problem. I'm sorry as well.'

'There, that wasn't so hard, was it?' said Father, beaming at us.

'No, Father,' Dilly and I said together, beaming at him.

We stopped smiling the second Father went through the door.

We watched TV for a while. Dilly sat in one corner of the sofa. I sat in the other, leaving as much distance between us as possible. I racked my brains for a way of proving the little horror had taken the family treat.

And then it came to me.

I remembered that odd expression on his

face, and realised I'd probably looked much the same when Mother had caught me on the landing. Dilly had felt *guilty* when Mother asked him if he'd been near the shopping!

I thought that if I made him feel even more guilty, he might own up and tell us what he'd done with our swamp-chocs. After all, I'd almost been ready to confess to Mother myself, and I hadn't done anything.

So that afternoon, whenever Mother and Father weren't around, I kept on at Dilly.

'Taking stuff which doesn't belong to you is called *stealing*, I said. 'And it's really bad. You never get away with it, either,' I added.

At first, Dilly pretended he wasn't bothered. But he didn't tell Mother and Father what I was saying, so I knew I was wearing him down.

'I'm not listening,' he said in the end, sticking his head under a cushion.

'It doesn't matter,' I said to his rear. 'I've decided to call the Dino-Police. They're good at catching dinosaurs . . . *who steal*.'

'You wouldn't do that . . . would you?' said Dilly's muffled voice.

I said I would, and that the Dino-Police would come and ask him lots of questions and take his paw-prints and prove he'd stolen the swamp-chocs, and then he'd have to go to prison, where he would stay for years and years and years without any pineapple juice or toys or TV, so there.

Dilly burrowed further under the cushion, his tail shivered and quivered the way it does when he's frightened . . . but he didn't

crack. 'Double drat,' I thought, convinced I'd lost. Then I stomped upstairs to sulk.

A little while later, Mother and Father were getting our tea ready when the doorbell went, ding dong. Dilly dashed to the door and opened it. And to our amazement, there in the porch was . . . a tall Dino-Police officer!

Dilly took one look at him and . . . that's right, you guessed it, he let rip with an ultra-special, 150-mile-per-hour super-scream, the sort that can blow a very surprised Dino-Police officer's helmet right off.

Then Dilly ran crying to Mother, scrambled up her dress, gripped her with his arms, legs *and* tail, and buried his snout in her neck.

'I did it, I stole the swamp-chocs,' he

wailed. 'I couldn't help it, they were in the hall when I came in, I hid them under my bed, I'm sorry, I'll never steal again, please, don't let him take me to prison like Dorla said . . .'

Whoops, I thought. It was time to disappear.

'Going somewhere, Dorla?' said Father. 'That's not very nice, especially when we've got a guest to greet. Dilly and Dorla, I'd like you to meet an old friend of mine. Donald's been in the Dino-Police for years . . .'

Of course, I hadn't called the Dino-Police, and Donald hadn't come to arrest Dilly, only to see Father and the rest of us.

Dilly felt rather silly when he realised he needn't have confessed to his crime. But the whole story had to come out. So we were *both* in trouble – Dilly for taking the swamp-chocs and me for frightening him.

We sat together on the sofa waiting to be told off.

'Well, what's the verdict then, Donald?' asked Father.

'Guilty as charged, I think,' Donald

replied, and laughed. 'But don't be too harsh on them. They seem pretty sorry, and I'm sure they'll promise to be *exceptionally* good from now on.' Dilly and I nodded eagerly.

'It's just a shame about the swamp-chocs,' said Mother wistfully. 'I was really looking forward to those this evening . . .'

'Perhaps I can help there,' said Donald, producing a box with a flourish from his pocket and giving it to Mother and Father. 'I bought these as a present for all of you . . . it looks like I chose just the right thing.'

'I'm afraid you'll have to go without, Dilly,' said Father after he'd thanked Donald, 'seeing as you've already scoffed a whole box yourself.'

'Actually, Father,' said Dilly with a big smile, 'I haven't had a chance to eat any yet. Er . . . could Dorla and I share them?'

Mother and Father laughed and said we could. And do you know, for a moment I almost felt that I wanted to hug my little brother.

It's terrible what a sweet tooth can do to you, isn't it?

DILLY SAVES THE DAY

'Hooray, we're going to see Aunt Darlene!' said Dilly. 'Are we nearly there yet, Mother? Are we? Are we?'

Dilly and I were strapped into the back seat of the dino-car and Mother was driving. As you can tell, Dilly was rather excited, although it was hardly surprising. Aunt Darlene is *definitely* one of his favourite relatives.

She's married to Father's younger brother, our Uncle Dan. I was a bridesmaid at their wedding and Dilly was a page. Now Aunt Darlene was expecting a baby dinosaur and she was due to lay her egg very soon.

'Just be patient, will you, Dilly?' replied
Mother. 'I can't help it if the roads are busy.
Why don't you ask Dorla to play Dino-Spy
with you?'

Dilly did just that and I said OK, so we
took turns for a while. But suddenly Dilly's
eyes widened and he pressed his snout to the
window.

'I spy with my dino-eye . . .' he said, 'the
place where Aunt Darlene lives!' Then he
yelled, '*YIPPEE! YIPPEE! YIPPEE!*' as
loudly as he could.

I clapped my paws over my ears to protect
them. Mother slammed on the brakes and
we screeched to a halt at the side of the

street. Mother turned to look at Dilly with that Enough-Is-Enough expression of hers.

'It *isn't* Uncle Dan and Aunt Darlene's block of flats, Dilly,' said Mother sternly. 'It's not even similar. And I'd be grateful if you didn't shout like that in the dino-car. You don't want us to have an accident, do you?'

'No, Mother,' said Dilly. 'I'm sorry.'

'That's all right,' said Mother. 'But how often must I tell you about your voice? I swear, sometimes it's just like a siren. The last thing Darlene needs at the moment is to have you making that sort of noise around her. Either you keep the volume *down*, or we don't go, OK?'

'But Aunt Darlene doesn't mind me being noisy,' said Dilly.

He did have a point. Aunt Darlene is lots of fun and she never complains about Dilly yelling and shouting, even when he deafens the rest of us. But things had changed, as Mother explained.

'Try to understand, Dilly,' she said as we moved off again. 'Darlene is in a, er . . .

delicate condition and shouldn't have any shocks. I dread to think *what* might happen if you make her jump.'

'Mother means the egg might start coming,' I said. 'I saw a film at school about the facts of life. There was this lady dinosaur, and she had an egg inside her just like Aunt Darlene, and she got a pain, and then . . .'

'OK, Dorla,' said Mother briskly. 'You can spare us the gory details.'

But now Dilly was looking even more excited than before.

'*Wow*, that would be terrific!' he said. 'I could watch. Hey, I could even help! It would be like an episode of *Dinosaur Hospital*, only in real life, with me, the brilliant Doctor Dilly saving Aunt Darlene and her egg . . .'

'It's nice of you to offer, Dilly,' said Mother, giving him a strange look in the rear-view mirror. 'But I doubt if there's anything *you* could do.'

'You don't know that,' snarled Dilly. 'You're only saying it because I'm young and

37

you're grown-up. It's just not fair the way you mothers and fathers think us small dinosaurs can't do things. You never, ever give us a proper chance, do you? We can though, can't we, Dorla?'

'Er . . .' I started to say, but Dilly swept on. He talked and talked and Mother and I had no choice but to listen. At last Dilly drew a deep breath.

'I *could* help if you'd let me, Mother,' he said. 'But you *won't*.'

Then he folded his arms with a . . . 'Humph!' and glared fiercely at the back of Mother's head. I was amazed she didn't instantly burst into flames.

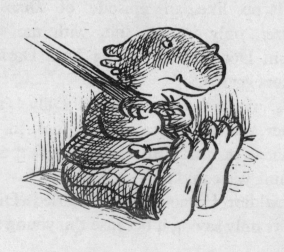

'*Well*, Dilly,' said Mother. 'That was quite some speech. I had no idea you felt so strongly about it. Mind you, I'm pretty sure we won't find out this afternoon which of us is right – seeing as you'll be on your best behaviour. And above all, you're gong to be *quiet* . . . aren't you?'

'Whatever you say, Mother,' Dilly muttered sulkily.

He was still sulking when we arrived at Uncle Dan and Aunt Darlene's block of flats. We went in the lift and he didn't insist on pressing the button for their floor like he always does, or on ringing their bell. And when Aunt Darlene opened the door, Dilly did something *very* silly.

'Why, hello!' said Aunt Darlene. 'It's lovely to see you! Come in, come in. Give me your coat, Dorla. And how are you, Dilly?'

'OK,' whispered Dilly so softly you could barely hear him.

'You don't sound it,' said Aunt Darlene, looking a little concerned. She put a paw on his shoulder. 'Have you got a sore throat?'

'No,' whispered Dilly. He stuck his snout

in the air and marched off towards the sitting room. 'I'm just being . . . *quiet*.'

Aunt Darlene looked at Mother, who rolled her eyes at the ceiling. Then she told Aunt Darlene about the conversation we'd had in the dino-car.

'Oh, I see,' said Aunt Darlene and smiled. 'I almost wish Dilly *would* startle me into laying my egg. I'd like to get it over with.'

Dilly was sitting next to Aunt Darlene on the sofa. When she said that, he looked at her and opened his mouth the way he does when he's going to scream. Mother and I both ducked . . . but nothing happened.

'Just kidding!' said Dilly. Then he and Aunt Darlene laughed, and soon Mother and I joined in. After that, Dilly didn't sulk or whisper any more.

To be honest, he behaved very well. He didn't make much noise, or spill the pineapple juice Aunt Darlene gave him, or eat too many fern-cookies, and he only asked a couple of embarrassing questions about her egg.

He wasn't naughty when Aunt Darlene

showed us the little nursery she and Uncle
Dan had got ready for their baby dinosaur,
either. And he didn't moan or whine when
Mother said we had to leave.

We said our goodbyes to Aunt Darlene at
the front door, and each of us gave her a kiss.
But then suddenly, she put her paws on her
tummy. She looked as if she were having a
pain . . . and she was.

'Oh dear,' she said nervously. 'I think the
egg is coming!'

'Don't blame me,' said Dilly quickly. 'I
didn't do anything!'

'OK, you mustn't panic, Darlene,' said
Mother, taking no notice of him. 'I'm sure
we've got plenty of time. I can drive you to
the hospital. Perhaps you'd better call Dan
and tell him to meet us there.'

Aunt Darlene did as Mother suggested.
Then we all went down in the lift to the
dino-car, Mother holding Aunt Darlene's
arm, me carrying her bag for the hospital,
and Dilly chattering with excitement.

We put on our seat belts and Mother
drove off.

'Just relax, Darlene,' she said reassuringly. I'd noticed Aunt Darlene *was* looking worried and seemed in quite a bit of pain. 'The hospital isn't far,' Mother added. 'We should be there in a few minutes.'

But Mother hadn't reckoned with the traffic. The roads had grown even busier since we'd arrived at Aunt Darlene's flat. We hadn't been going very long when we found ourselves stuck in a jam. We sat there for half an hour, with Aunt Darlene getting more and more agitated.

'Hang on, Darlene!' said Mother, patting Aunt Darlene's knee.

'I can't,' said Aunt Darlene anxiously. 'Oh, why won't those dino-cars move?' Mother tooted the horn, but nobody budged. 'We should have phoned for an ambulance,' said Aunt Darlene. 'Then we'd have a siren . . .'

'Oh-oh,' I thought. I remembered what Mother had said earlier. I glanced at Dilly and I knew immediately he had remembered it too. He had a big smile on his face, and if he'd been a cartoon character, he would have been sitting under a 'thinks' bubble with a light bulb inside it. He had an idea.

'We *have* got one, Aunt Darlene,' he said eagerly. 'Listen to *this* . . .'

'Dilly, don't you dare . . .' said Mother, turning round. But it was too late.

Dilly had already wound down his window and stuck his head out. He opened his mouth as wide as it would go and . . . that's right, you guessed it, he let rip with an ultra-special, 150-mile-per-hour super-scream, only this time he didn't stop, he went on, and on, and on.

At first Mother was furious. But then Aunt Darlene and I made her look at the

dino-cars in front. The drivers obviously thought Dilly's scream *was* a siren – and they were moving aside! Mother put her foot down, and we roared off to the hospital, with Dilly being our siren all the way . . .

We made it and so did Uncle Dan, who was there when Aunt Darlene laid her egg. Everything was fine, and within a week, a sweet baby dinosaur had hatched out. Uncle Dan and Aunt Darlene called her Daisy.

They also gave Dilly a large present when we went to visit them, and said that he was a real hero. He looked *very* pleased with himself.

A few days later, I overheard him talking to Mother.

'You see, Mother,' said Dilly. 'I told you small dinosaurs can help.'

'You were right, Dilly,' said Mother, 'so I was wondering if you'd like to help *me* – with the washing, the ironing, the cleaning . . .'

'Er . . . actually,' said Dilly, 'maybe there are *some* things I can't do.'

'That's funny,' Mother replied. 'I had a feeling you'd say that.'

And she was smiling as he scampered away . . .

Dilly and the Screaming Ban

'Tell Dilly we'd like a word with him, would you, Dorla?' said Mother one morning. She was ominously grim-faced, and so was Father.

'Oh boy,' I thought, rubbing my paws together as I went to fetch Dilly. There's nothing a big sister enjoys more than seeing her pest of a little brother get what he deserves and I had a feeling he was really in for it.

His ultra-special, 150-mile-per-hour super-scream has been out of control recently. He's been letting rip with it an awful lot, and I was pretty sure Mother and

Father had reached the end of their tether.

Dilly was watching TV, with the other main love of his life on his lap. I'm referring to Swampy, his pet swamp lizard, of course. He'd do *anything* for Swampy. Dilly didn't want to come, but I said he had to.

Father explained that he and Mother were fed up with Dilly's scream. He said Dilly was getting too old for that kind of behaviour, and even if *he* wasn't, *they* were. The moment had come to put a stop to it . . . for ever.

'Which means, Dilly, that as of today, your scream is totally, completely, and permanently forbidden,' said Father. 'Is that clear?'

'Whatever you say, Father,' replied Dilly, shrugging and turning to go.

Dilly obviously reckoned Mother and Father couldn't make a screaming ban stick. After all, they had banned him from doing lots of things in the past, and it had never worked. But this time they were *determined*.

'Hang on, Dilly,' said Mother. Dilly paused. 'There's something else you should know. We've decided that if you *do* scream again, you won't be allowed to watch any television . . . *for a whole month*.'

Dilly's eyes popped, his jaw dropped, and his tail went rigid. 'Phew,' I thought, I had to give my parents top marks on this one. Dilly couldn't live without television for a day, let alone a whole month.

'You . . . you . . . can't be serious,' he managed to stutter at last.

'We most certainly are, Dilly,' said Father.

Mother and Father had come up with a winner and Dilly knew it. So for the rest of the morning, he moped about with that I-Hate-Everybody-And Especially-My-Nasty-

Parents expression on his face.

I ignored him, but Mother and Father don't like it when he's in that sort of mood. They couldn't think of a way to bring him round though, so I suggested a visit to Dinosaur Park. It's one of our favourite places.

'What a wonderful idea, Dorla!' said Father. 'We could take a stroll over there after lunch. Is that all right with you, Dilly?'

'I suppose so,' said Dilly, trying not to sound too pleased.

'Why don't you bring Swampy?' said Mother. 'If you want my opinion, you could both do with some fresh air and exercise.'

Dilly didn't say another word . . . but now he couldn't stop himself from smiling. At lunchtime he gobbled down his food incredibly fast, and had his shoes on ages before Mother, Father and I had finished eating.

Swampy was just as keen. The second he saw Dilly holding his leash, he started scratching frantically at the front door. And when we set off, he shot out of the gate and

down the street, dragging Dilly behind him.

Dinosaur Park really is a terrific place. There's plenty of open space and a lake with paddle boats for hire. But the best part is the playground. It's got swings and slides and roundabouts and loads of climbing frames.

'Can we go to the playground first?' asked Dilly when we arrived.

'Yes, Dilly,' replied Father. 'But leave Swampy with your Mother and me, don't misbehave and remember – *no screaming*.'

'I will,' said Dilly. 'I mean, I won't. I mean, I promise I'll remember. Cross my heart and my eyes too, break my vow and smell like . . .'

'Er, thank you, Dilly,' said Father. 'I think you've made your point.'

'Race you, Dorla,' said Dilly. 'Last one there's a swamp snail!'

Dilly scampered off towards the playground and I chased after him. He had a head start, so by the time I got there, he had already disappeared into the crowd of young dinosaurs enjoying themselves inside.

That was fine by me. I didn't want to be bothered by my pesky little brother while I was having fun. I had a go on a roundabout and whooshed down The Diplodocus Slide, which was great. Then I went to the swings. Several dinosaurs were waiting for a turn, including Dilly.

Someone got off a swing and Dilly moved forward. But another little dinosaur pushed him aside and sat on the swing instead.

'Hey, I was next!' said Dilly indignantly.

The other little dinosaur simply stuck out his tongue and laughed.

Dilly looked cross, although there wasn't much he could do. Then someone else got off a different swing and Dilly was on it in a flash, giving the other little dinosaur a Yah-Boo-Sucks glare as he dashed past.

An alarm bell rang in my mind. Was Dilly going to start trouble?

But *he* wasn't the problem. It was the other little dinosaur, the one who had pushed in. Whatever Dilly wanted to go on, the other dinosaur got there before him, even if it meant jumping the queue.

I soon realised he was doing it deliberately to annoy Dilly. For some reason he thought it was hilariously funny and laughed at Dilly every time. That was bad enough. But worse was to come.

He began jostling Dilly and I could see Dilly wasn't cross any more, he was *angry*, and he was getting angrier with each shove. And usually, the angrier Dilly gets, the more likely it is that he'll use his secret weapon.

'He's going to scream any minute now,' I thought . . .

I was wrong. I could see he wanted to, but it seemed the prospect of a month without TV was just too much to bear. Dilly stayed silent and looked quite relieved when

Mother called us out of the playground.

'Would you two like an ice-cream?' she said.

Dilly and I said we would. So Dilly took Swampy's leash from Father and we walked over to the cafeteria by the lake. There we joined a long queue of dinosaurs waiting at the ice-cream counter.

'What are you having?' asked Father. 'OK . . . a Fern Feast for you, dear, a Mud Ice for me, a Lemon Swamp Pop for you, Dorla, and . . . *Dilly*,' he said suddenly, 'how often have I told you it's rude to stare?'

I turned to see who Dilly was staring at and my heart sank. It was the little dinosaur from the playground! He was behind us in the queue with a couple of grown-ups. They were probably his parents, I thought.

Father apologised for Dilly, and they smiled and said it didn't matter. Then the two sets of parents got rather chatty. But the little dinosaur and Dilly didn't. They made disgusting faces at each other instead.

It might have gone no further – *if* the little dinosaur hadn't realised that Swampy

belonged to Dilly. He must have done, for as
the queue moved along, I noticed him
edging closer and closer to Dilly's pet.

'Dilly . . .' I said, thinking I'd better
warn him. But I was too late.

The little dinosaur trod hard on Swampy's tail. Swampy squealed, Dilly whirled round, guessed what had happened, thought for a second . . .

Then opened his mouth wide to unleash an ultra-special, 150-mile-per-hour super-scream, the kind that flattens mean little dinosaurs, devastates ice-cream queues, and blows out three cafeteria windows.

I don't think I've ever seen Mother and Father so cross. They gave Dilly *such* a

telling-off. They went on and on at him and said he wouldn't be allowed to watch TV for the rest of his life, or maybe even a lot longer.

But he didn't seem to care, and they just didn't understand.

I did, though, and I knew I had to speak up. There's nothing a big sister likes better than seeing her pest of a little brother get what he deserves. But for once, he really didn't deserve what he was getting.

'Actually,' I said, during a brief lull. 'It wasn't Dilly's fault – it was *his*.'

I pointed at the little dinosaur, who was back on his feet. He was trying to look innocent, but his parents weren't fooled.

'And you *promised* you wouldn't be naughty today . . .' they said.

Apparently the little dinosaur had a bit of a reputation for being horrible and his parents believed every word when I told them what he'd done to Dilly and Swampy. So then there were lots more apologies.

The little dinosaur's parents made him say sorry to Dilly, Dilly said he had to say sorry to Swampy, Mother and Father said sorry to Dilly for telling him off, and then Father said sorry to the cafeteria manager.

She said it was all right, and that she would send us a bill.

And when we got home, Dilly *was* allowed to watch TV. Mind you, Mother and Father did say he should let them know in future if someone was being nasty to him at a playground, and *they* would deal with it.

'So am I still banned from screaming, Mother and Father?' he asked.

'Oh yes, Dilly,' they said together firmly. 'You most certainly *are*.'

Dilly just gave them one of those mysterious, We'll-See-About-That smiles of his and skipped off. Somehow I don't think that's the last we've heard of his ultra-special, 150-mile-per-hour super-scream.

But then Dilly wouldn't *be* Dilly without
it . . . would he?

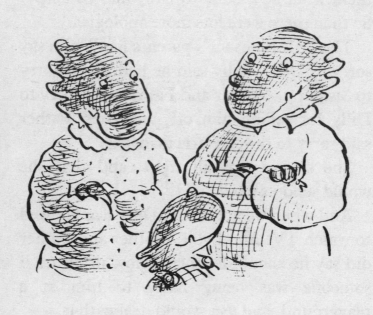